The Longest Home Run

Story by Roch Carrier

Illustrations by Sheldon Cohen

Translated and adapted from the
original French by Sheila Fischman

Tundra Books

The longest home run in the history of baseball was hit by a girl.

It happened right in our own village. We were playing in our usual field among the daisies. The girl just turned up.

"I want to play."

We were really surprised. Baseball was no game for girls. We'd never seen this stranger before.

"My name is Adeline."

We pretended we hadn't heard her. Then, as if she were a boy, as if she were on our team, she said: "It's my turn at bat."

She picked up the bat and walked to the plate. She waited for the ball. Her legs weren't even shaking, and she glared at the pitcher. The ball was thrown directly over the plate.

She smashed it.

The ball went flying. It seemed lost in the sky, forever, but a minute later we saw it above the shortstop. It sailed over the apple trees. Over the fence. It flew over the potatoes and past the cow grazing on the other side of the woodpiles.

Then the ball seemed to hesitate when it got to the window of Sergeant Bouton's house. It appeared to stop and think things over before it decided to keep going. The window pane shattered, exploding like a bomb.

Sergeant Bouton came outside. He screamed at us, but we were already running away.

Sergeant Bouton used to be a soldier. He stood straight as a sword. If anyone came near his property, he flew into a terrible rage. He waved his fists and shouted. Sergeant Bouton really scared us.

Adeline wasn't from our village, so she didn't know how terrible Sergeant Bouton's temper could be, but she ran faster than the rest of us through the daisies.

"What did you say your name was?" I asked.

"Adeline. I'm a magician. Come to the show tonight."

And then we understood. For a week now posters had been advertising the incredible show by The Great Ratabaga and his daughter, Princess Adeline.

We had all heard a powerful voice ring out over the rooftops crackling like a radio:

"Step right up, come one, come all, see the greatest magician in the world, The Great Ratabaga, and the Princess Adeline. We have come from the Orient on a magic carpet, bringing secrets that will turn the world's philosophy upside down."

All of us had seen the battered truck, patched together like an old sock, driving down our streets. None of our parents would dare be seen in such an old wreck. Fortunately, it was decorated with planets, stars, suns and half-moons. Suitcases were piled on the roof.

Adeline could hit the ball that far, all the way into Sergeant Bouton's window, because she was a magician. Or maybe a witch...

We were the first ones in line at the ticket window in the parish hall.

Both of our baseball teams sat in the second row. The red curtain stirred. Adeline must have seen us.

Soon the parish hall was filled with men in dark suits and with ladies wearing hats that looked like bowls of fruit.

We heard three knocks and then, in a cloud of smoke, The Great Ratabaga appeared. He wore a turban and had a thin moustache with points like knitting needles.

He brandished the longest sword. Slowly, carefully, he drove it into his belly. Then he turned around. We gasped as we saw the blade sticking out of his back. It gleamed in the light. We applauded very hard.

With the blade still stuck in his belly, Ratabaga announced: "And now, please welcome the Princess Adeline."

She had played baseball with us. She was our friend. We applauded.

On stage, Adeline didn't look the same. She had drawn red circles on her cheeks. Even her eyes were different: they were bigger now. She was wearing a kind of caftan and baggy pants. She was covered with sequins.

Adeline showed us her bare hands, palms down, palms up. As if it were the most natural thing in the world, she plucked roses from the air in front of her one after the other, and she offered her bouquet to the curé who sat in the front row.

"It's a miracle!" he cried.

The parish hall erupted in an avalanche of applause.

Like a real princess, Adeline curtsied. Then, standing very straight, she put her hands behind her back. Nothing seemed to be happening. Then we noticed a little flame on her lips. Like a bubble. As if she'd just blown up a red balloon.

The fire chief jumped to his feet. "It's against the law to play with fire in a public place!"

Delicately, Adeline took the ball of fire in her hands and bit into it like an apple.

It was amazing. Our two teams applauded our friend Adeline, harder than the rest of the audience. Adeline was indeed a great magician. No wonder she could hit the ball so far, right through Sergeant Bouton's window.

Just then, The Great Ratabaga came back on stage. He opened the lid of a big trunk, and shouted:

"Adeline!"

Adeline sat down inside the trunk, waved to us and bowed her head. The Great Ratabaga pulled down the lid. Then he uttered some magic words, opened the trunk again, and turned it on its side. Adeline had disappeared.

When the show was over, we waited for her in front of the drawn curtain. Everybody else had left the hall, but we were hoping to see our friend again.

Behind the curtain, there was a lot of activity; objects were being moved. We were getting restless because Adeline had not come back out.

"Maybe Adeline doesn't know we're waiting," I suggested.

"Go and tell her."

I was the shyest of us all but I always got picked for these difficult jobs. My friends stayed at the bottom of the little staircase that went backstage. I pushed open the door. The Great Ratabaga had taken off his turban. He was no taller now than any little man.

"Can I speak to Adeline?"

The Great Ratabaga gave me a look that made me sorry I'd asked the question.

"Adeline? I made her disappear. Didn't you see?"

We all set off for home. It was late; the July night was bright and riddled with stars.

I couldn't believe that Adeline had disappeared. We had old trunks in our house. Nothing ever disappeared from them. Quite the opposite. Old things had been kept in them for a hundred years.

Instead of going home, I went back to the parish hall.

I decided to spy on The Great Ratabaga's truck. I didn't have to wait long. From my hiding place in the cedar hedge, I saw the silhouette of Ratabaga carting boxes, objects, tables, swords. All at once I saw Adeline disappear into the truck, like a black cat in the night.

The next day, both of our teams were back in the field of daisies. Nobody dared to say so, but we were all hoping for Adeline to come back and play ball with us. I kept the secret about her disappearance to myself.

Our only problem was, we didn't have a ball. Adeline had made it disappear through Sergeant Bouton's window. And who do you suppose was picked to get the ball back?

My legs shook, my heart pounded as I rang Sergeant Bouton's doorbell. He greeted me with those steely eyes that had made the enemy tremble during the war.

"What do you want, you little pest?"

"I want my ball."

There was enough fire in the Sergeant's eyes to melt me. I couldn't move. I couldn't run away.

"Come in, my friend," I heard.

Sergeant Bouton had never called anyone "friend." Sergeant Bouton had never invited anyone into his house.

His house had an old smell, with old furniture, and old photographs on the walls.

"Here, take this and listen to me," said Sergeant Bouton.

It was chocolate. Sergeant Bouton had never offered chocolate to anyone.

He stuck under my nose the ball that he was hiding behind his back. "This ball that broke my window set a world record... How old are you?"

"I'm eleven."

"Eleven. My boy, you're going to become the world champion. You'll outshine Babe Ruth. I'll train you myself. Here, take your ball. Break all the windows in my house if you want..."

Sergeant Bouton was smiling. No one had ever seen Sergeant Bouton smile. I felt uncomfortable.

"My boy," he said, "I hope I live long enough to hear you on the radio giving the Yankees a good licking."

I couldn't keep the truth from him any longer. I took my ball and my chocolate and moved towards the door.

"It wasn't me that hit the ball," I confessed.

The Sergeant's smile vanished and his face went hard again.

"It wasn't me, it was Adeline..."

"And who is Adeline?"

"She's a girl."

"What? A girl! That's the end of the world!"

I ran for it. I was already far away but I could still hear Sergeant Bouton roaring:

"Pest! Bandit! I'll make your parents pay for my window!"

That happened a long time ago. From what they tell me, Adeline's record still stands.

For Raphael in California, who wishes he could read and play baseball. Unfortunately, he's not even one month old.
Roch Carrier

Sheldon Cohen dedicates his work in this book to the family of his childhood — his parents Rachel and Kelly, and his brother David.

Published in Canada by Tundra Books,
481 University Avenue, Toronto, Ontario M5G 2E9

Published in the United States by Tundra Books of Northern New York,
P.O. Box 1030, Plattsburgh, New York 12901

Library of Congress Catalog Number: 92-62364

National Library of Canada Cataloguing in Publication Data

Carrier, Roch, 1937 -
[Plus long circuit. English]
The longest home run

Translation of: Le plus long circuit.
ISBN 0-88776-312-X

I. Cohen, Sheldon, 1949 - . II. Fischman, Sheila. III. Title. IV. Title: Plus long circuit. English.

PS8505.A77P5613 2001   jC843'.54   C2001-930155-3
PZ7.C37Lo 2001

We acknowledge the support of the Canada Council for the Arts for our publishing program.

We acknowledge the financial support of the Government of Canada through the Book Publishing Industry Development Program for our publishing activities.

Printed in Hong Kong, China

1 2 3 4 5 6   06 05 04 03 02 01